W9-CGR-284

FELIX, THE FUNNY FOX

Written by Ski Michaels
Illustrated by Ben Mahan

Troll Associates

DORN MEDIA CENTER

Library of Congress Cataloging in Publication Data

——

    Felix, the funny fox.

    Summary: Felix the fox tries to make his new
neighbors like him by wearing funny faces and clothes.
    [1. Foxes—Fiction. 2. Behavior—Fiction.
3. Friendship—Fiction. 4. Neighborliness—Fiction]
I. Mahan, Ben, ill. II. Title.
PZ7.P3656Fe   1986   [E]   85-14097
ISBN 0-8167-0590-9 (lib. bdg.)
ISBN 0-8167-0591-7 (pbk.)

Copyright © 1986 by Troll Associates, Mahwah, New Jersey
All rights reserved. No part of this book may be used or
reproduced in any manner whatsoever without written
permission from the publisher.
Printed in the United States of America

10   9   8   7   6   5   4   3   2   1

FELIX,
THE FUNNY FOX

Felix Fox was new to the
neighborhood. He had just
moved in.
"What a nice neighborhood,"
Felix said.

"I like this neighborhood," said
Felix. "It looks like a friendly
neighborhood. And I like
friendly neighbors."

Felix was a friendly fox. He
liked having lots of friends.
Friends are nice to have.
Everyone needs friends.

Out went Felix to meet his
neighbors. Out he went to make
friends.

Did the neighbors want to make friends with Felix? No! Felix was a fox. And some foxes are not friendly. Some foxes hunt their neighbors.

Rob Rabbit was a neighbor. He
saw Felix. He did not know
Felix was nice.
"A fox!" said Rob. "Foxes hunt
rabbits."
Rob was afraid. He quickly ran
away.

"Stop, neighbor," yelled Felix.
"Do not be afraid. Do not run.
I am friendly."
But Rob did run. He did not
want to meet Felix.

Poor Felix Fox. He was sad. He
did not want the rabbit to be
afraid of him.

Another neighbor came by. The neighbor was Ken Quail. Ken saw Felix. Ken was afraid. "Yipes!" he yelled. "A fox. Foxes hunt quail."

Felix saw Ken Quail.
"Do not be afraid," said Felix.
"I am a new neighbor."
Ken Quail did not want a fox
for a neighbor. He ran away.

Poor, poor Felix. He did not
want his neighbors to run away.
But they did.

Which neighbor saw Felix next?
Mary Mouse did. Was she
afraid? Yes! Away she ran.

16

All the neighbors ran away.
They did not want to meet
Felix. They did not know Felix
was a friendly fox.

Poor, sad Felix.
"A new neighborhood is not nice
without friends," he said.

"I am not a bad fox," said Felix.
"I do not hunt my neighbors.
I do not want my neighbors to
be afraid. How can I make
friends?"
Felix thought. He thought and
thought. He thought of a way to
make friends.

Felix laughed.
"I will be funny," he said. "I
will make my neighbors laugh.
If they laugh, they will not be
afraid. If I am funny, they will
know I am nice."

How can a fox be funny? He
can look funny. He can wear
lots of funny things. And that is
what Felix did.

Felix Fox wore a funny nose.
It was a big, funny nose!
"This funny nose will make my
neighbors laugh," said Felix.
Felix went out. He went out
wearing the big, funny nose. He
went out in the neighborhood.

Rob Rabbit saw Felix. He saw
the big, funny nose. He was not
afraid. He did not run away.
He laughed.
"Look at that funny nose," Rob
said. "What a funny, funny
fox!"
He laughed and laughed.

That is how Felix met Rob.
That is how Rob and Felix
made friends.
"Felix, you are a funny fox,"
said Rob. "I like funny foxes."

The next day Felix went out. He wore the big, funny nose. He wore a big, funny hat. What a funny-looking fox he was!

Another neighbor saw Felix.
The neighbor was Ken Quail.
Ken saw the big, funny nose.
He saw the big, funny hat.

Was Ken Quail afraid? Did he run away? No! He laughed and laughed.

"That fox cannot be bad," he said. "He looks too funny to be bad."

That is how Felix and Ken
Quail made friends.
"I like having a funny fox for a
new neighbor," Ken said.

What did Felix do next? He
wore big, funny pants. He wore
the big, funny nose. He wore
the big, funny hat, too. Felix
went out in the neighborhood.

Which neighbor saw Felix next?
Mary Mouse did. Was she afraid
of the funny fox? Oh, no!
She laughed and laughed
and laughed.
"I like to laugh," Mary said to
Felix. "I like a funny fox."
That is how Mary Mouse met
Felix. That is how the new
neighbors made friends.

Day after day, Felix went out.
He always wore lots of funny-
looking things.
Felix wore a big, funny nose.
He wore a big, funny hat. He
wore big, funny pants. He wore
a funny wig.

Sometimes he wore a funny
shirt, too. Everyone laughed at
Felix.

But Felix was not laughing.
He was sad.
"Being funny is no fun," said
Felix. "I do not want to be funny
all the time."

Did Felix have to be funny all the time? Did he have to make his friends laugh? He thought he did.

He put on the nose and hat.
Felix put on the shirt and pants.
He put on the wig. And he put
on big, funny shoes. Out he
went.

The neighbors saw Felix.
"What a funny nose and hat,"
said Rob Rabbit.
He laughed.

"What a funny shirt! What
funny pants!" laughed Ken
Quail.

"What a funny wig!" said Mary
Mouse.
She laughed and laughed.

The big shoes were funny, too.
But they were too big. TRIP!
Felix fell.

The neighbors saw Felix trip.
They saw him fall. They stopped
laughing.
"Felix! Felix!" they yelled.

Felix laughed. He thought
tripping was funny. It was not
funny. It is not nice to laugh
when someone trips.

"Big shoes are not funny," said Rob Rabbit.

"They make you trip," said Ken
Quail.

"The funny shoes made you fall," said Mary Mouse. "Do not wear them."

"No funny shoes?" said Felix.
"Then how can I be funny all
the time?"

"You don't have to," said Rob.
"You are nice and friendly. We like you, funny or not."
"Yes," said Ken.
"Yes," said Mary.

FELIX FOX

"What a nice neighborhood,"
said Felix.
After that, Felix was not funny
all the time.

He was a funny fox just sometimes.